H̲omework

THE ANT AND THE GRASSHOPPER

Adapted by Janet Quinlan
Illustrated by Jason Wolff

Copyright © 2005 Publications International, Ltd.
All rights reserved.

This publication may not be reproduced in whole or in part by any means whatsoever without written permission from
Louis Weber, C.E.O., Publications International, Ltd., 7373 North Cicero Avenue, Lincolnwood, Illinois 60712
Ground Floor, 59 Gloucester Place, London W1U 8JJ

www.pilbooks.com

Permission is never granted for commercial purposes.

8 7 6 5 4 3 2 1
ISBN 1-4127-3761-3

Summer had just begun. Animals and insects scurried about, enjoying the warm weather. "Summer's here! The best time of the year!" the Grasshopper sang happily.

A line of ants marched past the Grasshopper, carrying small seeds and bits of food. As they walked along, some crumbs fell to the ground. Before the ants could retrieve them, the Grasshopper ate every last one!

An ant at the end of the line walked up to the Grasshopper. "We've worked very hard to gather this food," said the Ant. "You should have helped us pick up what we dropped."

"That's what's wrong with your summer song," the Grasshopper sang. "You work, work, work, all day long. Summertime is for playing, not working."

"Summertime is for planning and gathering," said the Ant. "It's time for getting all the food we'll need for the winter."

"Winter is so far away, I'd rather go outside and play," said the Grasshopper. He was about to hop away when the Ant stopped him.

"Wait! What about the food you took from us?" the Ant asked.

"Oh, yes. Thank you," said the Grasshopper, pointing toward a field. "And over there is a whole field of wheat to replace your crumbs. I like cornfields better myself, but that might be too far for you to walk." And with that, he hopped away.

The Grasshopper quickly forgot about the Ant and headed to the cornfield. He leaped onto a cornstalk, where a leaf made a soft bed. Above him, another leaf offered shade. And within reach, an ear of fresh corn gave him food.

"Those ants can gather, work, and store. I'll just snooze right here and snore," he thought to himself. Then he fell fast asleep.

Meanwhile, the rest of the animals in the woods were very busy. The squirrels stored their acorns, and the Ant lined the tunnels of his home with seeds and other foods. "When winter comes, we'll be snug and warm in our nest," thought the Ant.

All summer, the Grasshopper watched the ants. When he saw them going to a picnic for crumbs, he hopped along to eat his fill. While they carried food back to their nest, he slept in his cornstalk bed.

Then one day, the Grasshopper heard a loud noise in the field. The farmer was coming to harvest the corn! The Grasshopper jumped into the grass. "That was a close call," sang the Grasshopper. "Now I've lost my food and bed! I don't know where I'll rest my head."

A line of ants was marching past and heard the Grasshopper. The Ant stopped. "The days are getting shorter, my friend. But there is still time for you to store food and find a winter shelter."

The Grasshopper thought about that for a second.

"Not today, I've got to play," he sang, and hopped his way through the grass.

The Grasshopper frowned. The sun was setting, and it was getting chilly. In the distance, the farmer was cutting hay. "Doesn't anybody here know when to play?" he asked aloud.

He hopped off to the apple orchard. Most of the leaves were gone from the tree. But the Grasshopper found a few small apples on the ground. He munched on them until he was full. Then he settled in for a nap near the root of the tree. The Grasshopper shivered. He looked around for a sunny spot, but the sun was already gone from the sky. "Someone needs to tell the sun that its working day is not done," he sang unhappily.

The sun was one thing the Grasshopper didn't mind seeing at work. With each day, though, it seemed to work less and less.

The ground seemed colder, too. And one day, when the Grasshopper tried to nibble an apple, he found that it was frozen. "I don't like my apple in ice," said the Grasshopper. He was so shivery, he couldn't think of a second line to his rhyme. "Ice, nice, rice, mice…"

"Hmmm," he thought. "Mice. That's a good idea. Maybe I'll visit my friends the mice. I'll bet it's warm and cheerful in their snug nest."

It was indeed, and the Mouse family was delighted to see the Grasshopper.

"Thank you for visiting, Mr. Grasshopper," said Mother Mouse. "I would invite you to stay, but all of my sisters and brothers are moving in for the winter. Isn't that wonderful? Oh, here they are now!"

A crowd of mice rushed into the nest. It was nice to see them hugging each other. But the Grasshopper was hoping to find a place to stay for the winter and a bite to eat. He was out of luck at the Mouse house.

Disappointed, the Grasshopper hopped back to the orchard. The ground was so cold that it hurt his tiny feet. "Where are those ants, now that I need them?" he sang sadly.

Snow began to fall. It covered the Grasshopper, and he fluttered his wings to clear it away.

He had to get inside or he would freeze! Hopping as fast as he could, the Grasshopper raced to the Ant's house. "Is anybody home?" he called as he stepped into the tunnels.

"Why aren't you outside, playing in the snow?" asked the wise Ant.

The Grasshopper wanted to say that he had just come by for a visit. But he could feel the cold wind on his back. Sadly, the Grasshopper sang, "I should have listened to what you said. Now I'm cold and scared and unfed." It wasn't his best song, but he hoped the Ant would understand.

The Ant did understand. But he wanted to be sure that the Grasshopper understood, too. "We got our food for the winter by working hard. If you stay with us this winter, you'll have to work hard, too."

The Grasshopper gulped. Months of hard work sounded difficult. Would he be able to do it? Then he remembered the snow and ice outside, and he made up his mind to try.

"If you will only let me stay, I will work all night and all day," sang the Grasshopper.

"Wonderful," said the Ant. "Your job here will be to sing for us every day." He laughed. "Because winter is our time to play."

So the Grasshopper sang for the Ant and his family all winter long. And the following summer, the Grasshopper sang a song as he helped to gather food. "Summer work is slow and steady. But when winter comes, I'll be ready!"

Hard Work

The ants in this story work very hard all summer, gathering food for the long winter ahead. They take pleasure in doing their job well. Because they plan ahead, they are able to play, and enjoy the winter.

On the other hand, the Grasshopper chooses to play all summer, and he has no food or shelter when the weather gets colder. The ants teach the Grasshopper that there is a time for work and a time for play, and each makes the other possible.